To librarians, who always know where to find things
P. R.

For Franny, who always knows where the moose is
R. C.

Text copyright © 2006 by Phyllis Root
Illustrations copyright © 2006 by Randy Cecil

First edition 2006

Library of Congress Cataloging-in-Publication Data

Root, Phyllis.
Looking for a moose / Phyllis Root ; illustrated by Randy Cecil—1st ed.
p. cm.
Summary: Four children set off into the woods to find a moose.
ISBN-13: 978-0-7636-2005-9
ISBN-10: 0-7636-2005-X
[1. Moose—Fiction. 2. Stories in rhyme.] I. Cecil, Randy, ill. II. Title.
PZ8.3.R667Loo 2006
[E]—dc22   2006042581

2 4 6 8 10 9 7 5 3

Printed in China

This book was typeset in GothicBlond.
The illustrations were done in oil.

Candlewick Press
2067 Massachusetts Avenue
Cambridge, Massachusetts 02140

visit us at www.candlewick.com

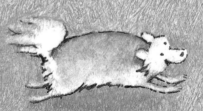

Looking for a
MOOSE

Phyllis Root

illustrated by Randy Cecil

CANDLEWICK PRESS
CAMBRIDGE, MASSACHUSETTS

"Have you ever seen a moose—
a long-leggy moose—
a branchy-antler,
dinner-diving,
bulgy-nose
moose?"

"No! We've never, ever, ever, ever, ever seen a moose. And we really, really, really, really want to see a moose."

"Let's go!"
We put on our hats.
We pull on our boots.

We look in the woods—
TROMP STOMP!
TROMP STOMP!—
the treesy-breezy, tilty-stilty,
wobbly-knobbly woods.

We look and we look,
but it's just no use.
We don't see any long-leggy moose.
"Now what?"

"We'll look in the swamp
for a dinner-diving moose!"
We roll up our pants.
We take off our boots.

We wade in the swamp—

squeech squooch!
squeech squooch!—

the sloppy-gloppy, lily-loppy,
slurpy-glurpy swamp.

We look and we look,
   but it's just no use.
We don't see any long-leggy,
   dinner-diving moose.

"Now what?"

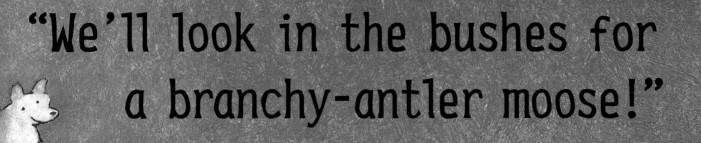

"We'll look in the bushes for
a branchy-antler moose!"

We roll down our pants.
We button up our sleeves.

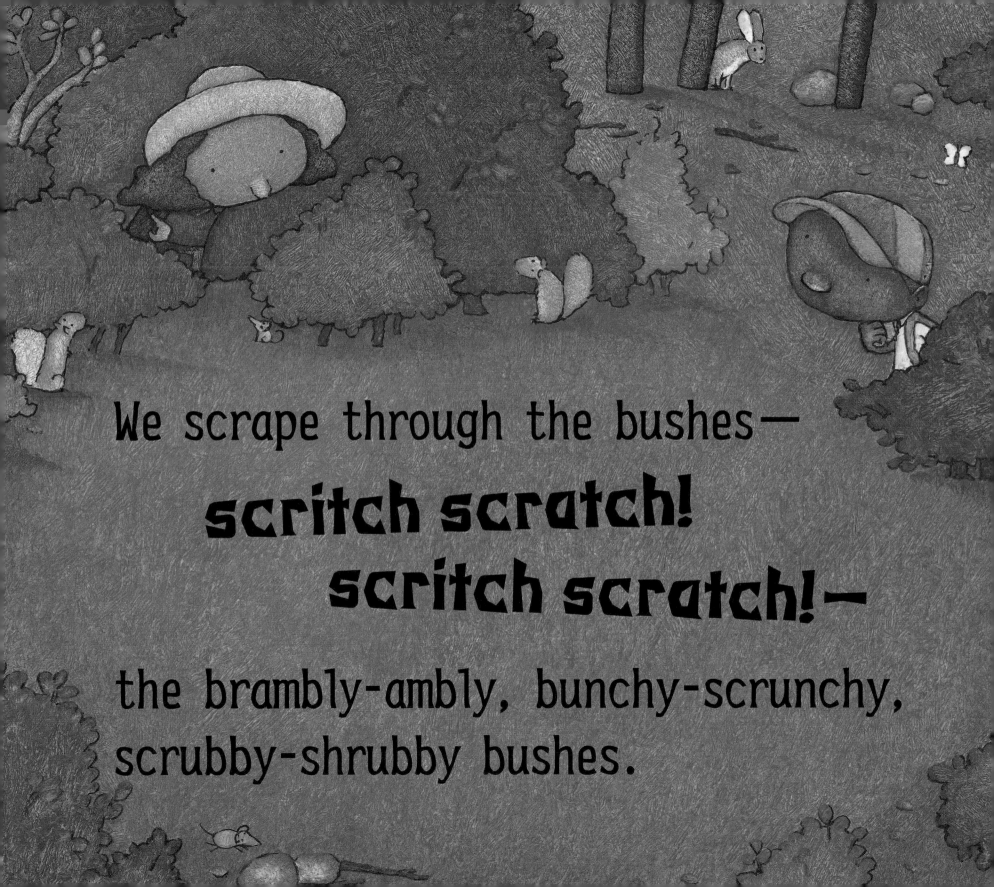

We scrape through the bushes—

scritch scratch!
scritch scratch!—

the brambly-ambly, bunchy-scrunchy,
scrubby-shrubby bushes.

We look and we look,
   but it's just no use.
We don't see any long-leggy,
   dinner-diving,
      branchy-antler moose.

"We'll look on the hillside for
a bulgy-nose moose!"

We take off our hats.
We tighten up our packs.

We scramble up the hillside—
TRIP TROP! TRIP TROP!—
the rocky-blocky, lumpy-bumpy,
fuzzy-muzzy hillside.

We look and we look,
   but it's just no use.
"We'll never, ever, ever, ever,
      ever see a moose!"

"What's that?"

"LOOK THERE!
It's a long-leggy,
dinner-diving,
branchy-antler,
bulgy-nose moose . . .

and a moose . . .
    and a moose . . . .

and a moose."

"We've never, ever,
ever seen so many
moose!"

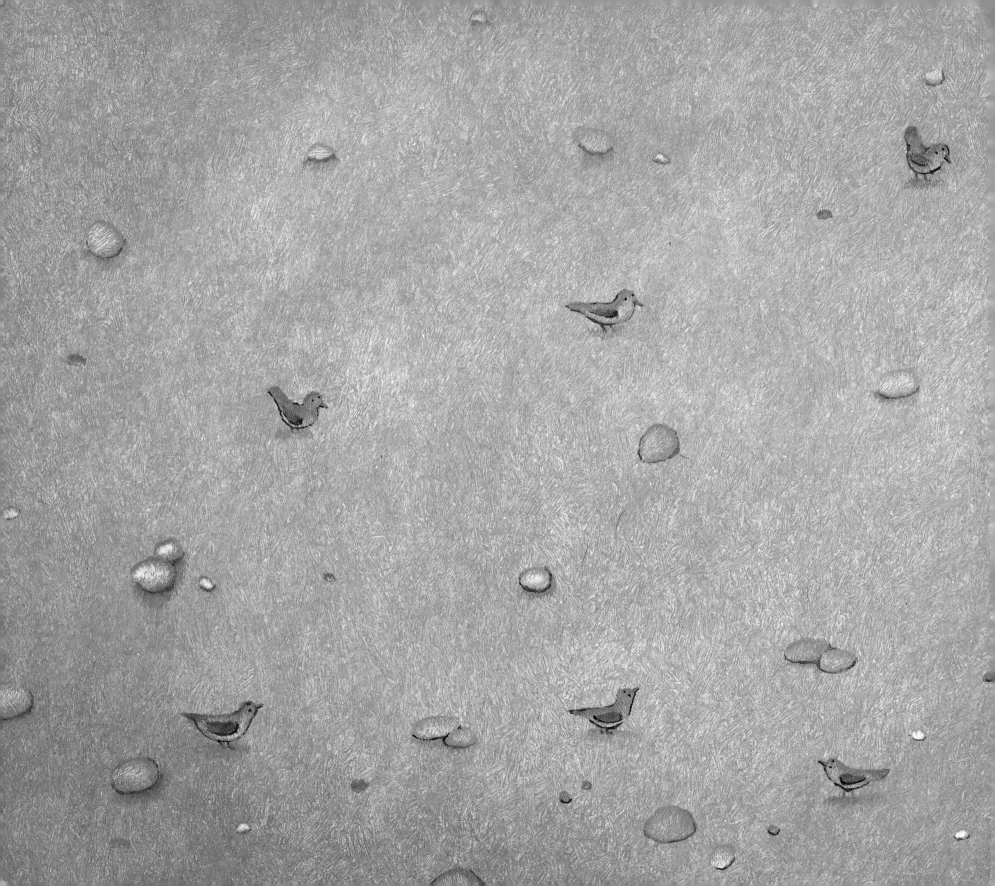